ART, MYSTERY

MAYO THOMPSON

ART, MYSTERY

DRAG CITY | CHICAGO

DC665

No resemblance to situations or persons
living or dead is unintentional.

Request to make copies of any part
of this work must be mailed to:
Permissions Department,
Drag City, P.O. Box 476867,
Chicago, Illinois 60647-6867,
or emailed to:
info@dragcity.com.

Drag City Web Address:
www.dragcity.com

Printed in the United States of America
Library of Congress Control Number: 2017940777
ISBN: 978-1-937112-20-2

First Edition

For
Maria,
Marilyn,
Mustafa,
&
Ferdl

1

Ring-ring.

"Hello?"

"Mr. Tile, Mr. Perlat Tile?"

A foreign man.

"Pablo Pablon calling."

"Who?"

"Mr. Tile! Please — Bern! 'Eighty-seven!"

"Oh — right — okay."

"I am looking for an export agent. I found your listing online. You are an export agent now, no?"

"Si, Señor."

In his mind's eye Tile saw again Pablon's red card, and relived imagining kicking his head into space when he stuck it around the office door, but the adrenal rush was gone.

Things had grown abstract.

"Please, have a seat. What can I do for you, Señor Pablo?"

"Pablon — I am an art handler."

"Ah-ha."

"For a while now."

"And you want to export a work of art?"

"I do."

"I specialize in chrome."

"But you can handle things, no? Legally, I mean. You are licensed to handle any durable good, no?"

"I am that."

"Well then."

"There are agents specializing in art."

"Perhaps but I — well — you — there is a reason why you. Please."

Pablon handed over a folder, photocopies of two pages of H.W. Janson's *History of Art*, the business card of a local art gallery — Gallery Harmoni — paper-clipped to one corner.

Top plate page one showed a Cellini portrait bust, the plate below, a statuette — "Hercules and Antæus," by Antonio Pollaiuolo, from around fourteen-hundred-seventy-five, bronze, forty-five and a bit centimeters in height, now in the National Museum in Florence.

Hercules had Antæus clear of the ground.

Hercules and Antæus, Antonio del Pollaiuolo

The plate on the other page was Antonio's "Battle of Ten Naked Men" — a Pulitzer bequest to New York's Metropolitan Museum of Art, an engraving, from somewhere between fourteen-hundred-sixty-five and fourteen-hundred-seventy. The title covered it.

"I want to export a Pollaiuolo statuette."

"Like the one in the picture?"

"Yes, but there's — I don't have it yet."

"Oh — Look — get it, and — for old time's sake — to let bygones be bygones — I'll do your paperwork. How's that?"

"Very generous — but — getting it depends on you."

"Sorry?"

"I need you to get it."

"Señor?"

"You are key to acquiring it."

"I am — ?"

"Key."

"Key?"

"I believe so."

"How?"

"Your asking will set things in motion."

"My asking who or whom?"

"See the card? Visit the gallery. That will get the ball rolling."

"What do I say?"

"Start with the artist's name."

"Assuming I agree, what would I be looking for?"

Pablon had the adventure clincher: a faded photograph of what he claimed was a Pollaiuolo statuette: a bronze, two men again, quite close in likeness to "Hercules and Antæus," but not fighting...

2

It was stupid of course. But there was a hum to it, and a sense of consequence. He hadn't felt either since he couldn't remember when without dredging up stuff.

And there was money in it.

He went to call on the gallery.

He walked. It was nice out, chilly, and blowing so hard occasionally that he had to hold onto his hat.

Three or four blocks before the street to the gallery — he wasn't counting — he came up behind a big woman, tall, striding along on shapely legs. In olden days his impulse would have been to accelerate with the idea of catching up, tipping his hat, saying hello etc. Today he slowed to her pace, listening to the rhythm of her heels, taking in the way she negotiated pedestrian traffic, wasn't fussed by it, gust or bluster, was spectacular.

His street approached. She was angling that way too.

The wind took his hat. While he was chasing it, she was all ease, clutching her billowing cape, riding it sidewise on the wind, tacking majestically into the very street.

He felt not a little let down when he made the corner and she was nowhere to be seen.

The gallery wasn't far along.

Ignoring a sign reading, 'closed', Tile tried the heavy glass door. It was open.

The space was big for the neighborhood, high-ceilinged, dark.

The walls were white and blank.

At the back a modern looking desk stood beside a sliding door tall and wide enough to drive a half-ton truck through.

He strolled towards it, footfalls echoing his presence.

As he approached, sure enough the big door rattled and slid open enough for a young man to lean half through.

"Sorry. Didn't you see the sign? We're closed for installation."

Tile neared, hands in pockets, stopped at a non-threatening distance, smiled, rattled his keys and change.

"I saw it."

The emptiness of the street struck him.

"The lady? Who just came in? I'd like to speak to her, please."

"Do you have an appointment?"

"No."

"You need an appointment."

"It won't take a minute."

"No one sees Ms. Jasmine without an appointment."

At the obvious pleasure in the look on Tile's face upon hearing the lady's name, the young man bit his lower lip.

"No matter what?"

"Pardon?"

The young man blushed and brushed back a fallen lock. Tile felt for him.

"Mind?"

He stood at the desk, took out his chrome-plated ballpoint and waggled it between two fingers so that it looked as if made of rubber, grinned at the kid, produced one of his business cards, wrote 'Pollaiuolo' on the back, crossed and gave it to him.

"I've got business. Make me an appointment, please?"

The lad took the card, read both sides, sighed, looked back at him.

"Just a minute."

"Please."

He withdrew and slid the door to.

Tile put away his pen, then frisked the desk, looking for literature.

It was empty.

The door opened, but barely a jot.

One of the boy's eyes was in it, wide, frightened. His voice squeaked.

"Leave at once or Ms. Jasmine will call the police."

Tile didn't know what to think. He eyed the eye, blinking in the crack, shrugged and left.

Maybe he'd been surveilled going through their drawers.

He telephoned Pablon.

"This isn't going to work. I went to the gallery — tried to see the lady in charge but she wouldn't see me. I spooked her."

"Spooked her?"

"Made her nervous. Something. She said leave or she'd call the cops."

"My word! But wait — I thought you said you weren't able to see her?"

"I did — I wasn't. She didn't say 'leave' herself. Look, she knew I was there, and she knew why. I wrote it on the back of one of my cards. Okay, sorry, this is a bit confusing. It was like this: I asked the kid working there if I could speak to the lady in charge. He said I needed an appointment. I wrote 'A. Pollaiuolo' on the back of one of my cards, gave it to him, asked him to make me an appointment. I figured she'd see what was up, come out, we'd talk. Instead, the kid came back, said she'd call the cops if I didn't leave, so I left."

"But — since you didn't see her — how did you know she was there?"

"Okay. Back up. Earlier, when I was heading for her place, so was she, at the same time. I came up behind her in the street. She made the corner where the gallery is and was inside before I made the corner — it's the first door. When I asked the kid about seeing her I was just guessing."

"Oh."

"By the way, that gallery doesn't look like showing art made before the Twentieth Century."

"What a gallery shows does not always represent all and only what it handles."

"Oh."

3

Tile obviously had things to learn.

Before he had time to think about how a gallery could handle things outside representation his doorbell rang.

Two cops in plain clothes.

They looked like street thugs.

“What’s up?”

“Why are you stalking the lady?”

“What?”

“You shouldn’t be stalking the lady.”

“Yeah, generally. Stalking ladies ain’t allowed.”

“Stalking?”

“The lady says you followed her.”

“You’re talking about the lady from the gallery?”

“Who else?”

“I happened to come up behind her in the street.”

“That’s not what she says.”

“You followed her.”

"To her place of business."

"I wasn't following her in the sense she suggests. Really. I'd no idea where I was going was where she was going. Or that where I was going was her place of business. She made the corner before I did."

"You asked for her — "

" — tried to see her."

"I wanted to talk to somebody in authority — "

"You didn't ask for no 'authority'. She says you asked for her."

"It was a guess. Intuition. I asked myself, 'could the lady in the street belong to the gallery?' As I said, she made the corner before I did. When I made the corner, the street was empty. I wasn't surprised at not seeing her. I wasn't thinking about it. There are shops for classy ladies in that street. I was on my way to the gallery."

"What for?"

"Business."

"And some little bird said, ask for the lady."

"Right."

"What business?"

"An art object."

"You?"

"Since when did you get interested in art objects?"

"You shuffle papers for chrome brokers."

"Historically, but not only."

They looked up at him hard.

"Listen, stay away from the lady. Understood?"

He looked down at them.

"Sure I understand."

He didn't understand.

He rang Pablon.

"This really isn't going to work."

"What? Why?"

"The police just visited, said stay away from the lady."

"The police? My goodness. I guess you did 'spook' her, as you said."

"I guess. What now?"

"I don't know."

"Why don't you talk to her?"

"It would affect the price in a way that your representing me as an anonymous buyer potentially avoids."

"Oh."

"Look. Try one more time? Perhaps you will be able persevering to convince her that you are interested in the statuette? Think you can do that?"

"I don't know."

4

Next morning instead of to the gallery, he went to see Naj — his only friend from football.

Naj had been team trainer, and a major in the secret police. When things came unstuck, he survived. In the new order, he thrived, finding uses for who and what he knew, and for his know-how. Critics and detractors said he was a gangster. He was a businessman whose empire included an entertainment complex in the old city, the first attraction behind a wall of reinforced concrete and steel, high and strong enough to keep King Kong in or out.

It was too early for the front door. Tile approached the backdoor doorman.

"Naj around?"

"You're?"

Tile handed him a card. He read it and looked him up and down. A light went on. He spoke to his lapel radio, listened.

"Right."

He squared up to Tile so his body-cam could see him. Pretty soon, he was leading him through a couple of doors, down a corridor, through a door marked NO EXIT, down a flight of concrete stairs to a passageway with security doors at both ends.

Tile'd seen the far one often from the other side. It opened directly on the dance floor of the currently empty subterranean disco-bar he sometimes drank in, normally entering the way of most flesh.

"Wait here."

The thug went away. Tile's shoulders sagged to normal.

In a moment, steps, and Naj appeared out of nowhere.

"Perly, boy?"

"Najocchio."

"You aren't usually on the razzle this early, old son. To what do I owe this morning's visit?"

"Last night? I had a heat wave?"

"Over what?"

"Stalking, they said."

"Stalking? You?"

"That's what I said — stalking? — me?"

"Who were they from?"

"No idea. They were young — thirty somethings. Number one was about your size, a hipster, gray military surplus overcoat, stringy, dirty-blonde hair, stubble, chinos, ostrich cowboy boots. Number two was a throwback — a prole, mullet, green jacket — some kind of reptile — Converse All Stars — also green."

"Hm. Sound like boys from Narco, maybe. Funny suchlike being sent to visit you. What'd they say?"

"Stay away from the lady."

"Sounds like boyfriend stuff."

They sat in a booth off the bar.

"What's her name?"

"Ms. Jasmine. Don't know her first name."

"What'd you do to her?"

"Went to her gallery."

"What gallery?"

"Harmoni."

"Hm. What kind of gallery?"

"Art."

"Commercial? Or picture?"

"Commercial."

"What's she got you want?"

"I think she's got something I want."

"Think — okay. What's she got?"

"A statuette — Italian, Renaissance."

"So what happened?"

"I'm not sure. She told them I followed her. I can see why she might have thought that. I was on my way to her gallery when she was too — I came up behind her in the street. Just before the street the gallery's in I lost my hat — it was windy. By the time I made the corner, she wasn't there. I went to the gallery. I was talking to a kid who works there when something said, ask to see the lady. You know me. I chanced it. The kid said I'd need an appointment. I gave him a card to give her. I thought she'd pop out and talk. He came back, spooked, said she'd call the cops. Maybe I scared her. Also maybe — while he was in the back I frisked the desk. Maybe they have cameras? Anyway, I left."

Naj smiling, tutted.

"Perly, Perly. Since when did you get interested in art?"

He laughed when Tile told him how he'd always been in a way, and how he came to be.

He roared when Tile told him about the statuette.

"And somebody's ready to pay for that?"

"Si, Señor."

"I'll be."

5

Mid-evening, hoping to make peace and do business, he drove over to the tower Ms. Jasmine couldn't say enough wonderful about living in on social media.

It was swanky.

His presence was rewarded when a big aubergine Mercedes pulled up in the forecourt. The front door burst open and a doorman emerged, stood to one side holding it while tipping his peaked cap at Ms. Jasmine.

She passed without acknowledging him, a small man holding her by one elbow.

The driver was out in a flash, a burly youth in a dark suit, rounding the big machine and opening the back door.

The guy was trying to steer her but losing. He was also trying to explain something. That wasn't going well either.

Five meters out the door she rounded on him, and stepped to him.

She towered over him. He cringed, took a half-step back, gloved hands up to protect his head. Would she crown him?

She folded her arms and just looked at him.

He smiled, sheepishly, squirmed, tried a little laugh, made a contrite face, inched towards her, carefully, reached, up, to touch her hard-set chin, talking softly the while.

She raised it, twisted 'round and showed him her back.

He scowled.

Time stood still. What was he going to do?

Eventually, realization set in. His face fell. He looked to the doorman, the driver, the doorman. Both sympathized. Neither dared commiserate.

He sighed. They were right of course. It was hopeless.

He shrugged, turned, resigned, strayed to the car, paused at the door, looked back, sighed again, ducked in. The driver closed the door gently but firmly, went around, mounted up, put her in gear, let go the brake, and drove slowly away.

Tile half expected to see the guy's face in the rear window.

She must have hoped the same. When he looked to see what she was doing, she was flipping off the parting car.

With a certain self-satisfaction, she snorted, the warm air through her flared nostrils condensing in the cold night air. She signaled the doorman.

He came, stood to attention, listened closely, tipped his peaked cap, turned, and began running up the street towards the intersection with the main road to find her a taxi.

Tile dismounted, buttoned his coat, looked both ways, crossed the street, and strolled over, and up to her.

She was transfixed, seeing him coming on like that. Her eyes narrowed, darted, side to side — looking for somewhere to escape to.

Ultimately she saw of course there was nothing for it but to just stand there and wait.

He knew how she felt.

She would be steaming mad, of course.

He tipped his hat, smiling broadly.

"Ms. Jasmine?"

Her expression soured, mouth and brow curving darkly at the sound of his making something savory of her name.

"How dare you! Go away. I'll call the police."

"Again? Wait, please. Please? Wait?"

She folded her arms, patted her foot. How he disgusted her. She looked away — up the road for the doorman, the damned taxi, defiance in her face, shifting her weight from foot to foot. She squinted, why didn't he just go away?

"Need a lift? I could drop you?"

He gestured back over his shoulder at his car. She sneered, started away.

He let her go for a bit.

"So? Antonio Pollaiuolo?"

She stopped.

Her shoulders went up. She fumed a good second, spun on a heel and marched up to him.

She could almost look him straight in the eye.

He tried keeping his eyes light, cool, amused.

Hers flashed ire. Her full lips compressed to a thin, quivering, pink stripe of pure exasperation mixed of what? Hatred? Fear?

He would have wished. She looked about to slap him. Would she?

"What do you mean? How dare you? Who are you?"

"Taking the last one first, you saw my card."

"I threw it away."

A lie.

"The cops?"

"What do you want?"

"I'm interested in acquiring the Pollaiuolo statuette word says you have."

"What? Word? What word? Where on Earth did you hear that?"

He showed the gallery card, and was happy with the effect. She was taken aback, and when she seemed almost to be thinking to reach for it, he snapped, and flicked it, like the ace of spades in a trick, and put it back in his vest pocket.

"I found it in an art history book on the Pollaiuolo page?"

"And putting one and one together, got three."

"In case you really did throw my card away permit me to give you another — we can do business."

He fetched and handed her another with a little flourish. She watched this with amusement.

It turned out to be at herself.

She took his card with a smirk, and ripped it in pieces, letting them fall like snowflakes.

This was getting good.

He looked at the bits scattered on the pavement between them, and was about to say something funny about her shoes when the doorman ran up smiling and pointing back. He was being followed by a taxi.

She smiled witheringly, waved thanks with her little black clutch at the doorman, and growled.

"Leave me alone, jerk."

With that she trotted to the taxi, knees-together, her skirt being that tight. She had a hot ass.

Like the jerk she imagined him to be, he trotted to his car, swung around and followed her.

The taxi took her back through town, to the Art Academy. He parked while she paid, then followed her in.

The place smelled of chalk, paint and disinfectant.

She stopped by the door of a studio and waved. Pretty soon a woman around his age came and spoke to her. She was nice looking, if severe, in black leather — small, thin, confident.

Through the door students with big pads looked up at a naked young man posed on a platform. He bore an uncanny resemblance to the Merc driver.

The women broke out laughing over something.

Eventually they kissed each other on both cheeks and parted. Ms. Jasmine took a taxi to the gallery.

He gave up, rang Pablon.

> "I finally managed to say 'Antonio Pollaiuolo' to the lady from the gallery."
>
> "Grand. And."
>
> "I can't tell if she knows what I'm talking about?"
>
> "Why do you say that?"
>
> "I don't know. Maybe it's me. You need to talk to her yourself."

Pablon said nothing.

"Are you sure about the Pollaiuolo?"

"What do you mean?"

"About its being there?"

"I don't know that it's at the gallery. I'm confident however that it will be produced now — now that she sees you are interested in it, not her."

What would it take to convince her, or himself, strictly speaking, of the latter?

6

He needed info — who collected Renaissance stuff.

Around lunchtime, instead of going back to the gallery to try just one more time, he drove over to the National Museum.

Reception in the administrative offices was empty but for the echo of a voice down one hall.

He went that way.

Someone on the 'phone.

> "...relatively. Absolutely. Of course — I am — It will — I don't think so — I'm confident — On grounds — You have my word on that...no...yes. Yes, perhaps they can be, but only narrowly — Listen! — quite. I was going to say, 'contingent' but 'esthetic' will do. I...all right. Until then. Good-bye."

Was this luck?

The voice turned out to come from the office of the Assistant Curator, Renaissance Art — just the man he was looking for.

Tile rapped lightly on the open office doorjamb.

The owner of the voice was mid-to-late forties, a doughy-faced man plainly not happy at his hulking presence filling the only way out.

Tile rounded his shoulders and stooped, holding his hat by the brim with just the tips of the fingers of both hands in a pose of classic obsequiousness.

It made the man's sense of his looming worse. He piped, trying to find his official voice.

> "How did you get in here? Where is Security?"

He reached for his phone.

Tile gestured back over his shoulder, and took a baby step in, spoke slowly, timidly.

> "There's nobody. It's lunchtime. Sorry. Sir — please? I have a wonder? About work by an artist from the Renaissance? Your specialty, I believe?"

> "You'll have to make an appointment. I consult strictly by appointment — Hello? Hello? — Damn."

He put his phone down. There was no one in the lobby.

> "It's okay. I'm sorry. I understand. You speak when engaged."

> "Exactly."

> "I should go. Try someday to make an appointment."

The exchange calmed him. He leaned forward, looking at Tile, and somewhere reprocessing and finding favor in Tile's knowing what he meant, swept his hand benignly through space.

"Try the internet. You'll surely find what you are after."

"I'm not after information so much — "

"Virtually everything anybody ever said or wrote — "

"Or stuff people have said, or written. I want to find one work."

Direct hit?

"Find one Renaissance work?"

"I've surfed. Plenty. Looked at everything I could find on the artist."

"Which one?"

"Pollaiuolo — Antonio Pollaiuolo."

The Assistant Curator looked down again, started to shift some papers. What was that? Blinking?

"We have no holdings."

"I know."

He looked up again.

"I don't believe I'm going to be of any help."

"Really?"

Tile looked at him so as to convey that he believed what he was saying but wasn't really so sure he couldn't be of help, looked down, rotating his hat, fingers inching along the brim, sighed lightly.

"You know Pollaiuolo's stuff?"

"I know it of course."

"Yes. But it isn't expertise I'm after? It's info."

"Info?"

"About collections, and collectors."

"Try Public Records."

His tone let it be known that he had lost interest in Tile's little problem.

Footsteps came down the hall towards them.

"Vari? Mr. Vari? Are you in?"

It was an older fellow, manicured, probably pedicured, surely pedigreed.

"Oh, sorry, Vari, didn't know you'd company."

"Not company exactly, Dr. Giorgio."

"Good day, Sir. Dr. Giorgio, Senior Curator."

"He's looking for information. I've said I can't help."

"Good day, Sir. Yes. He said he can't help."

Dr. Giorgio looked over his glasses at Mr. Vari.

"When a member of the public asks for help, I believe we should try."

"He's not looking for art help. He wants information."

"No, Sir. It's right. I am looking for collectors."

"What?"

"He's looking for a collector of works by Antonio Pollaiuolo."

"Antonio — What? Here?"

"It's right."

"There are none in this country."

"Information I have says differently."

"I beg your pardon?"

"Is it for sure that nobody here ever collected anything like that?"

"He's after information about art collectors, art collections."

"Try the National Archive."

"Mr. Vari suggested Public Records."

"Grand idea. Even better. Good luck."

There was a bit more, back and forth, going nowhere.

He left feeling uneasy.

He rang Pablon.

"What makes you think I can help you?"

"You were a fixture in the world of relations that brought the statuette here. It is still here."

"I don't know. Over at the museum they don't think so."

"The musuem?"

"I asked in the Renaissance department if they'd ever heard of anybody here collecting Pollauiolo. They said no."

"They did?"

"From the way they talked they were telling me to knock myself out if I wanted to, check Public Records or the National Archive."

"I've looked. Weren't we going to approach the gallery lady one more time?"

7

The gallery and the lady would have to keep until morning. He went back to Naj's, again by the backdoor, and was led to his office. Again, the way was funny.

The faint, dull, persistent thump said they were near the disco-bar.

Under the stadium Naj had added a personal touch to his office with décor and furnishings. Potted plants, flags, and a big Chinese rug made an impression, but there was no getting away from its being a windowless cinderblock cubicle with team-colored walls, or that his desk was so big it made one feel like company, two a crowd.

This one was also windowless, but spacious, paneled, and, instead of fluorescent, nicely lit.

The desk was gone. Naj's new workstation was a Biedermeier table, giant, with only a powerbook and a phone on it. The potted plants were gone too but not the Chinese rug. It finally looked at home spread out between the table and the door.

Like at the old office, photographs covered the wall behind Naj. Some but not all athletes, patrons, politicians, and folk heroes from the stadium had made the transition. Those that had were complemented by a legion of fat cat businessmen, sports stars, media personalities, film and pop stars, friends and associates, alone, in groups, around tables, smiling, toasting, on the dance floor etc. Some were autographed. Naj was in many, a friendly gorilla, beaming somewhere amidst. Tile was sure that his old self was there, possibly too his current one.

"Any luck with the lady?"

"Very little. Also — something funny — I can't find anybody who knows who the cops who visited you are, or work for."

"She must really know somebody."

"Could be somebody who knows somebody."

"That's a big help."

"Records says she comes from a village near Macedonia."

"Holy Cleopatra."

"The gallery is owned by Dr. Enver Harmoni. He drinks here — a football fan. I've known him since back in the day. He was a junior minister at Sport and Culture."

Tile raised his eyes to the wall.

"Dr.? He up there?"

"For sure. Let's see — "

"Anything on the statuette?"

"Word's out — how much is it worth?"

"No idea. I'm still trying to imagine how a Pollaiuolo could have gotten here."

"We have history with Italy."

"You think?"

"Maybe war booty? Bad old King Zog?"

"Any idea where it is?"

"You don't think that gallery has it? There he is!"

It was him all right, a quite dapper fellow, his generation.

"I think I need a doctor's appointment."

8

Knock-knock.

"Hello, wise guy."

"Fellows?"

"We come in?"

"I don't see why we ask. He has no manners."

"It's the law, colleague."

"We told you, don't pester the lady."

"I wasn't there to pester her."

"You came up to her in the street outside where she lives."

"I wanted to explain, and apologize. I want to do business with her."

"My ass."

"Take it easy."

"This guy gets my goat. You think anybody believes that?"

"Oh, please try."

"Why, you...."

"Hey, of all things, you shouldn't be trying to piss him off."

"Who's trying? From the aroma, he pisses himself."

"You big piece of — you're asking for it — he's asking for it!"

"Easy. You are pushing it, friend."

"Friend?"

"Yeah, friend. You should be nice to us. We're modern. We're trying to be nice."

"Oh, well. If it's like that."

"Look at me. This is your last warning. Do we make ourselves clear? Leave — the — lady — a — lone."

They gave him an array of ominous and knowing looks, cinematic, dire, fateful.

His line was easy.

"Gee, no need to get heavy."

They smiled at him, looked at each other, smiled, looked back at him, stopped smiling.

Number one growled.

"You're smart. Be smart. Keep your head."

9

Was he smart?

Keeping his head?

Sorting denotation in normal conversation was straightforward. The responsibility of each locutor is understood to be to try to communicate in as few uncertain terms as possible what the other is responsible for trying to take as seriously as possible. Processing in both cases begins with, and largely consists of applying common sense to expressions understood as not intended to deceive.

He couldn't rule her out, nor could he say that she was being deceptive. Her being mad at her boyfriend maybe had nothing to do with Pollaiuolo.

Ring-ring.

"Naj? What's up?"

"Dr. Harmoni's at the bar."

Tile bellied up in no time. Pretty soon they were chatting.

Tile couldn't help liking the guy. Unlike his girlfriend, he was open, approachable.

Softly softly. He stuck out his hand.

"Tile, Perlat Tile."

"Enver Harmoni — Wow! I'm damned! Of course! Oh, my goodness — The Beast of Bern. I'm honored."

"You're kind."

"Not at all. And now?"

"Export."

"Export."

"Export. You?"

"Art."

"Art's interesting."

"I have a gallery. Drop by sometime. My card."

"Thanks. What do you show?"

"Predominately Western Contemporary."

"I'll drop by."

"Do. What do you export?"

"Chrome. Lately I've started branching out, though. I'm actually looking to handle some art. I understand that there's money to be made. And I've gotten looking at it too, studying a bit. It's fun to look at and think about."

"And there is money."

"It's a new thing for me though. I'm just getting started. When I get looking I find angles, but so many I don't know how to get them in anything like a proper order."

"Angles on object relations is the game. Order is where you find it, or need it."

"Then I guess I'm playing, but I have loads of questions. Sometimes nothing but. Basic stuff. What makes an object a work of art? Are there things that are art objects *a priori*?"

"I don't believe so. Art is an abstract concept. Function consists of representations on terms, their entailments, and extensions."

"Explained in terms of want or need — "

" — subjectivity sublimates form in an esthetic interval in and on whatever terms necessary."

The Dr.'s voice was a nicotine-coated ruin, the ashtray his rhetorical prop — stubbing, flicking, crushing out, ingrained, nuanced.

Discourse went here, there, all over the place.

There were lulls of course. Following one where the Dr. stared into his drink for awhile, he emerged lamenting feeling cynical. What had become of the idealistic sensibility he enjoyed in youth?

"I mutated?"

There was one off-key moment when what turned out to be an old acquaintance of the Dr.'s came up behind him and tapped him hard on the shoulder.

Seeing who in the mirror behind the bar, the Dr. sighed, closed his eyes, and gestured wanly.

"Sorry—gave at the office."

The guy stood his ground.

Finally the Dr. twisted 'round on his stool and looked him up and down, eyebrow arched.

He snorted, swiped the back of his hand under his nose, sniffed.

"Ali?"

"Enver!"

"I thought so. Just my luck. Dr. Ali Faqu kneeling before me. Oh, you're standing."

Dr. Faqu was shorter than Dr. Harmoni, but a fire-hydrant rather than a floor lamp. He winked at Tile.

"That your best shot anymore?"

"Why should I waste my time?"

"Come on. Try again."

"Ali and I go way back, to Party parties— "

"Try. Come on. You're the lip."

"— taking *mons veneris* by strategy. Apropos of fucking, Ali, old boy, how is Cynthia?"

Dr. Ali bristled.

"She's fine, fuck you very much."

Dr. Harmoni went suddenly red.

"STILL PROFESSING?"

Dr. Faqu sneered loudly.

"STILL A SALESMAN?"

"PROUD OF IT!"

Applause broke out among some businessmen nearby. Dr. Harmoni gestured graciously, bowing to them from the waist.

Naj appeared.

"Gentlemen, please."

"Of course, Naj. Of course. Good-bye, Ali."

Dr. Harmoni swiveled back to face the bar, In the mirror, Dr. Faqu flipped him off. He laughed, glanced sidewise at Tile and Naj, shook his head at the sad predictability of the whole thing, smiled thinly, took a breath, returning to Earth.

"I've been rather expansive. Not too, I hope. How about that, Naj?"

"You're all right."

"Well, well, well, well, well. Bartender, a fresh round, please. Well, well. Join us in a little something, Naj? I never saw you standing still, you know? You were always moving — defending — running, punching, slapping, kicking, whatever it took."

"That's what I did."

"That is what he did."

"Really. Stand up, please. Let me have a look at you. You really filled the net."

Around three Tile followed him out. The Dr. pulled on gloves, signaled. His big Merc started up nearby.

"Going my way?"

"No, thanks. I'm right here."

"Leave it. It's early yet. I need to drop by my gallery, then we can hit Zenophobia or Tiranasaurus Tex. Whatever. We'll bring you back, or drop you at home."

He got in, intent on trying to discover something about the statuette.

Gallery Harmoni's back room was jammed with stuff — in crates, shadowy shapes wrapped in plastic, bins of mylar- and bubble-wrapped things in frames, leaning against one another, paintings, but no statuette gestalts.

The driver came up from the basement with a padded envelope. His eyes met Tile's. He smiled. Tile winked and nodded.

"Thank you, Hugo. Oh, and, Hugo, champagne please."

Dr. Harmoni reached a big pair of scissors, snipped, and there was a book — *Induction*. He clutched it greedily in both hands, face, a pleased child's.

"A classic."

He passed over the gray paperback, sub-titled 'Processes of Inference, Learning, and Discovery'.

Hugo came back with a bottle of champagne, opened it and filled flutes.

"Cheers."

"Cheers."

"Hugo, thank you, and help yourself. One glass only though. We'll move on. It's a first printing. A friend from America sent it. I could've ordered it of course but it's nicer this way, more friendly."

"Right friendly. Looks like something reading might do me some good."

"I can't say for certain but probably so."

"You know Pollaiuolo? Antonio Pollaiuolo?"

"A little. I saw 'Martyrdom of St. Sebastian' in London."

"Never been to London. I saw it in *The Story of Art*."

"I've read that."

Martyrdom of St. Sebastian, Antonio and Piero del Pollaiuolo

"It's attributed to Antonio, but nowadays his brother is credited too, and you see them called the 'del Pollaiuolos' — the Poulterers. What's going on there?"

"Gombrich was going on the information as it stood? Antonio's and Piero's collaborating must have been discovered since *The Story of Art*. Do you know Antonio's 'Battle of the nudes'? Or his 'David'?"

"'David', no. 'Battle of the nudes' fits the description of something I saw in *History of Art* — H.W. Janson? He calls it 'Battle of ten naked men'."

"Must be the same. I've seen it called, 'Battle of ten nude gods'. 'David' is worth seeing. If you happen to visit Berlin, it's in the Gemäldegalerie."

"Never been to Berlin."

"What about Gombrich's analysis of 'Martyrdom'?"

"Read it."

"Did it strike you at all how he treats it? Comparing it to 'Last Supper' and 'Galatea'?"

"How it's his stalking horse? It is different."

"It is. But these are horses for courses of course. 'Last Supper' and 'Galatea' are murals. 'Martyrdom' is an icon."

"The formal comparisons seemed legitimate enough."

(rotated) *Last Supper*, Leonardo da Vinci

Galatea, Raphael Sanzio

"They are. I just disagree with his gloss. In his Popperesque set-up, 'Martyrdom' is a failed conjecture, and 'Last Supper' and 'Galatea' refutations. The disjoints he adduces to prove his point are functions of his treating all three as attempts at accurately mirroring nature where the measure is seamless illusion, and 'Martyrdom' has seams. Artists may have shared a bag of tricks, and potential effects, social, political, and philosophical concerns, but theory, like style, was mediated, not least in relation to a contract — pace Baxandall. Read him yet?"

"He's on my list."

"His painting and experience book tells how Florentines enjoyed parsing and quantifying over specificity, entertaining ideas, appreciating order. Items functioned in a way like texts. In that regard, 'Last Supper' can be read as an image of the taste and interests of the monks who ordered it. The same goes for the tastes and interests of 'Galatea''s commissionaire. And, I would think, ditto those of whoever is behind the 'Martyrdom' altarpiece. Sebastian is his avatar."

"Interesting choice."

"Juicy isn't it? I can't help wonder at the ways in which his having been a trusted member of the imperial guard played in relation to the political economy of Florence, a very violent place. The del Pollaiuolos were commissioned to conjure the event no Florentine would fail to recognize, in this way. In real time, on the terrain of quotidian contradiction, the mode of execution is iconic."

"Funny how the icon relations are treated, and how Sebastian's martyrdom is fudged — his not dying of his wounds."

"Delicious. His being recognized at all is shown to depend on this event in his life, rather than his clubbing. Gombrich is that close to putting together how the painting works on its own terms. He's got all the bits. He recognizes the masterly handling and rendering. He sees how the composition is split, how the historic event is superimposed on the contemporary landscape but can't imagine that it's done deliberately, and knowingly. He says something like, 'there's no way from the promontory to the scenery below'. Quite. The historic event is superimposed on the contemporary landscape. 'Martyrdom' is an essay on Sebastian's iconicity. The main event referring unambiguously to the Crucifixion trope? For my money, that immediate recognizability gets the icon dialectic rolling. Epiphany is reached for working paired registers — sacred and profane, yesterday and today, abstract and real — reconciling ambiguity through faith. A man is tied to a pole and being shot full of arrows for some reason. The faithful see Sebastian's predicament for what it is, and know why.

As Jesus' was on the Cross, Sebastian's gaze is upward, to God, who, in this instance, is outside the painting, above and beyond its top edge. He is in his house, where the altarpiece stands. Within the picture he is present only to Sebastian and the viewer who can read. Unless you know the story, 'Last Supper' is just a dinner party gone sour. Whoever they are, again, as Gombrich sees rightly, and says, the main man is calm, fairly glowing, while the others are dismayed for some reason, and one no longer feels welcome. As in 'Martyrdom', the potential for piety derives from how one knows the picture. Gombrich is just stuck on illusionism. That reminds me, why did you ask about Antonio?"

"I was hoping you'd say, 'funny you should mention him'."

"You mean you want one?"

"Is there one?"

"I don't know of any. Hm. Well, well, well, well, well. That's interesting. Good luck."

Around five they went to Zenophobia.

"You know what I like about 'Martrydom'?"

"Gnn..."

"The archers are busy with their business."

"They're all the same guy."

"Sebastian too. Right? He was somebody."

At sunup they hit Tiranasaurus Tex. One drink in, he hit the wall.

"Dr.?"

"Sir?"

"I bid you goodnight."

"Well. All right, then. Goodnight."

"Thank you."

"Thank you."

"See you at Naj's."

"See you there."

Before hitting the hay, he tried Pablon. He'd have to tell him there'd be no getting the statuette from the gallery.

Pablon continued to encourage him about the gallery. Tile didn't know what to think, or say.

"It's your money I'm spending, running around."

"That's quite all right. By the way — "

"I don't see any future in this."

"No, no. I believe it won't be long before you make real progress. By the way — "

"Si, Señor?"

"I have relatives here, and, well, sadly, a dear cousin who lived here has passed."

"Gee. Sorry."

"Thank you. I can only be glad that I happened to be here just now. I'll want to export his remains. We've a family crypt in Italy. Do you think you could organize the paperwork, please? I'd be extremely grateful, and you would be compensated for that too of course."

"Sure. No problem. Will he be in a coffin?"

"No. In an urn."

"Drop by the office after lunch."

"Thank you."

10

Ring-ring.

"Hello."

"Mr. Tile, Ms. Jasmine."

"Woah — Ms. Jasmine, hello."

"Spare me smarm, and goo, and irony."

"I beg your pardon. I am genuinely surprised, pleasantly — delighted, to hear your voice."

"Save the sweet-talk too. I'm ready to talk about the statuette."

"You are?"

"My place. Now or never."

Thinking — she hadn't mentioned him to Dr. Harmoni. Would he be there too?

His heart thundered.

He performed a hasty but careful toilet, put on some nice clothes, jumped in his car, and soon was there. The doorman took him to the concierge who showed him to the lift.

Her floor was near the top.

The apartment was grand, open plan, with magnificent views over the city and the land beyond. Bathed in late sunlight, both had the charm of being distant.

They were alone. She led him to an area off the kitchen.

The erotic fantasy he had been nursing off and on since he first saw her was undiminished by her sheer distaste.

"Coffee?"

"Please."

"Stop staring."

"Was I? Sorry."

"You're burning holes in my breasts."

"Sorry."

"Well?"

"What do you mean?"

"You know very well what I mean. Tell me about the statuette."

"What? Tell you about it? I thought you had it."

"Obviously."

"Then you don't know who has it either."

"No. But apparently you do."

"I don't get that."

He looked down, blushed, looked up. She grinned. Had he given the game away?

His balls tingled.

"I have seen a photograph."

Her chin rose and her breasts pointed at him.

"And?"

Her eyes shone.

"What is it of?"

"A couple locked in erotic embrace."

"Wow."

"It looks a bit like 'Hercules and Antæus'?"

"What is that?"

"Another statuette by the same guy, ostensibly. You know the story?"

"No."

"Hercules has to wrestle Antæus. He gets his strength from his mother. She's Earth."

"Hercules holds Antæus clear of mother, he wins."

"Exactly. Here, I don't know if it's supposed to be Hercules again, but there's a big guy on the ground and he has hold of a little guy who is kind of up in the air — "

" — Hold it. 'Big guy', 'little guy'? Homosexual intercourse?"

"It's a funny pose but it works. There's penetration."

"Wow. How big is it?"

"Hard to say, looks about halfway in."

"Don't be impertinent. How big is the statuette?"

"Hard to tell from the snap. If it's anything like 'Hercules and Antæus', it's about this high."

"Fantastic."

"Why do you want it? I can guess why the guy I'm working for is interested but you? It's a bit too too for art in general, don't you think?"

"Exhibiting it would pose special problems but nothing insurmountable. There would be ways of handling it."

"Now who's being impertinent? What's it worth?"

"Ask Antiques Roadshow."

"Hahaha. Good one. No, really — what museum can show it?"

"Are you serious?"

"Yes. You can't let children in."

"You are a yokel."

"Maybe. But this whole thing's got me thinking, about art — know what I mean?"

"Take it easy. You don't want your brain overheating."

"I didn't think you thought I have one."

"Right, keep your reflex instinct in check."

"I like how you said, 'we' before. You and I doing business, assuming we can find, and get, the statuette, how would that work?"

"What do you mean?"

"Well, as you rightly said, there's the guy who hired me to find it for him. And of course there's your boyfriend? I gather you haven't mentioned me. Have you? Maybe I don't say anything to the guy I'm working for."

"I beg your pardon?"

"We keep quiet — find the statuette — "

"About my boyfriend — what did you say?"

"We bumped into each other, the other night. We got talking about art. When I brought up the del Pollaiuolos, he was blank, a clean slate."

"You what?"

"I was still thinking you two had it. Funny."

"When was this?"

"Night before last. At Naj's."

"At Naj's? Do me a favor?"

"Name it."

"Fuck fucking off."

"But I thought you needed me."

"That'll be the day."

11

Dr. Ali and Cynthia Faqu went to Tiranasaurus Tex to see and hear The Skipit Club, a girl-group from Kosovo.

Cynthia went straight to the bar.

Dr. Ali would like to have but got buttonholed by the art-director of a culture rag he was in cahoots with, worried about hitting deadlines for a photo-essay of scenesters in the latest Italian fashions for which he was thinking Arte Povera.

When he got to the bar, Cynthia was studying the bicep of a young man who modeled for her at the academy. He'd flex, she'd giggle, they'd laugh. Dr. Ali needed a drink.

The band was late. The sound system was humming. He spotted some of his students, some of hers. The hum stopped and the lights came up on 'The Prole' — emcee, artist, actor, once Cynthia's studio-assistant. He prowled the stage with a mic on a line.

> "Hello. Hallo. Abend. Ja, na, und, testing, testing, testing, one, one, one, ein, zwei, zwei, zzzzzwei, d, d, d, drei, fier, fear, sick, sick, sicker, hallo. Testing. Et cetera. Et cetera. Mary had a little blam, a little bling, a little cough, a little sting, a little...Okay. Even better. O. K. Yeah. Yay-uh. There. There. Good. All right. All

right. All right. Ladies, gentlemen, and — We...Excuse me? I...I'm what? — Nobody's ever said that before! Heh-heh-heh. Sure. After the show. Your place and mine. Anyhow, Ls and Gs, Bs and Gs, Ambiguities...it's time. OKOKOKO — SKIPIT CLUB!"

While the crowd cheered, he put the mic on its stand, turned to the wings and held his hands up for high fives. But the band came on cold, surly, gave him dirty looks. His face fell. His arms dropped. He looked puzzled. What was wrong? The singer told him. His face became a mask of sorrow. He apologized and slunk off. She shrugged, walked over and talked to the bassist and drummer.

When they were ready she came to the mic and said quietly, "We're *The*...Skipit Club. 1, 2, 3 — 4!

"We believe in love.

Yeah yeah yeah.

We believe in hate.

Yeah yeah yeah.

We have reasons.

Yeah yeah yeah.

We can explain.

Yeah yeah yeah.

But we won't.

No no no.

You wouldn't understand.

No no no.

How could you?

Yeah yeah yeah.

We're alien.

From a foreign land.

Yeah yeah yeah."

Halfway in Dr. Ali looked for Cynthia. She was nowhere to be seen. The young man too.

He sighed. He'd go home.

On the sidewalk he found Djmitri Djmitri, a fellow painter. He had a young woman on each arm. They were waiting for a taxi.

"My dear Dr. Faqu? We've had it. How goes it?"

"Totally cool. You?"

"Awesome. Totally."

"And who are these ladies?"

"These babies are Bebe and Kiki — meet Dr. Ali Faqu, artist, professor, old comrade. Join us. We're heading for Naj's."

Kiki and Bebe curtsied.

"Pleased to meet you."

One had a joke.

"Ding dong."

"Who's who?"

"Wrong."

"Not 'who's who' — 'who's there?'"

"Oh. Sorry. Who's there?"

"Witch."

"Which who?"

"Not 'which who?' — 'which witch.'"

"Which witch!"

"Oh — Sorry — Which which?"

"Witch Hazel!"

"Which which Hazel?"

"Which witch we're not buying!"

It didn't make sense but they fell about anyway. Maybe that was the sense.

The one who turned out to be Bebe draped herself around DD. Kiki smiled, told him they weren't sisters by blood.

"We're Seoul sisters. Know what Seoul sisters are?"

"Something to do with black music?"

"Korean nuns!"

A taxi pulled up. They all squeezed in the back.

"You in school, Kiki?"

"Not any fucking more. I'm a dancer. Let's dance."

At Naj's, they danced. The floor was crowded and hot. He flung his arms about, brushing her here and there with the back of a hand. She moved in close and grabbed him. He pirouetted away, giggling. Cocktails had made him giddy.

She came from behind, locked her body against his and humped him. She was hearty. They fell over. The number ended. People applauded. They got up and sat.

Bebe and DD smoked a big spliff. Kiki got it, put it in her mouth fire first, aimed the mouthpiece at Dr. Ali and blew a thick stream of smoke at him through the mouthpiece.

Bebe shouted.

"INHALE, BILL!"

The lights moved, the music throbbed, the mob dazzled. Dr. Ali's brain was weaving. He lit a cigarette. Kiki came and sat on his lap, wriggling deep, rolling around. She lay his hand on her puffy little tummy. He smiled broadly.

He needed to piss.

He and DD went and locked themselves in a men's room stall. DD laid out lines of Nextasy — designed to induce the sense that the present is the future.

"Benjamin Franklin! Seems a good guy. Why was he never President of the United States, in Congress or their Senate?"

"He never fucking ran."

"That says something."

While they were washing up, in came Tile.

Dr. Ali was transfixed. He knew all about Tile. Seeing him on the stool next to Enver Harmoni — of all damned people — that was a shock — lucky bastard. If asked he would have to admit he felt envious.

He longed to speak. Etiquette said no.

Nothing about Tile's way or look suggested he recognized him.

"Evening."

"Gentlemen."

DD elbowed the drier and began vigorously rubbing his hands, his rings clicking and clacking. He grinned at Ali in the mirror.

Dr. Ali shut the tap, took over the blower.

Tile came to the sink and washed his hands.

DD's and Ali's bloods rushed — Kiki burst in with the spliff.

At first they were paralyzed. She laughed, sized up Tile.

"Hi."

"Hello."

"Hit?"

"No, thanks."

Dr. Ali gathered his senses, took one of her arms, DD the other. They led her out.

Tile followed.

She got away from DD, locked on Ali and hung from his neck.

Tile went back to the bar.

They went back to their table.

Kiki wanted to sit on his lap some more. He took her on his knee instead, and reached for his drink.

"The future's looking bright. Bright bright. DD let's go to my place."

"Cool. What say girls?"

"Yes."

"Naturally."

"Just a minute. I'm going to invite someone."

12

Tile remembered Dr. Ali. He had seen him with the funny girl. Next thing he knew, here he was, headed his way, a funny look on his face.

"Excuse me, please. Mr. Tile?"

"Sir?"

"You remember me? Ali Faqu? We weren't introduced but I saw you when I said hello to Enver Harmoni? The other night?"

"I remember."

"I'm a big fan."

"Thanks."

"It wasn't very nice what happened of course — me and Enver. I came up to him at all really because I wanted to greet you and pay my respects. If I'd seen him alone — and I do in here from time to time — I'd have left it alone. But seeing you...well, I took a chance. I've seen you here too but never — well — I hope you weren't offended."

"None of my business."

"Listen. What about joining our party? At my place."

"Thank you. I don't know anybody."

"It's okay okay okay."

Ms. Jasmine's reaction suggested there might be more to Dr. Harmoni than face values he'd shown. A little background research might help.

"Well, if you're sure."

"I am. I am. I am."

Tile drove. They all happily piled in.

Dr. Ali's set up was a former workshop/storehouse on the outskirts of town. They sat on divans around a low table surrounded by tropical plants under grow-lights. It was warm and easy going.

The girls turned to Tile.

"What do you do?"

"Didn't you used to play football?"

"I used to. I'm an ex-sport."

"Ha ha ha."

"We like jokes."

"I'm an agent."

"Show-business?"

"No — "

"Secret?"

"Real-estate?"

"No — Historical."

"Historical?"

"Just joking. I'm in export."

"Ex-sport export."

"I should rename my business."

"You're nice."

"I can be."

"What's back there?"

"Take a look. Exercise room. Sauna; shower; wooden tub. The lot."

"Sauna?! Turn it on! Turn it on!"

"It takes awhile."

"So what?"

"TURN IT ON! PLEASE?"

"Okay."

"YAY!"

"Let's go look."

"You go."

Dr. Ali commanded the sauna to start and headed for the kitchen.

"I'll organize something to drink."

"Don't take too long."

"Don't worry."

"You guys are artists?"

"We are."

While the Scandinavian rocks got hot, Dr. Ali served drinks, then made DD help him shift canvases so he could show Tile his latest series.

There were ten pictures, all views of the National Museum. Each had a time of day, season, weather. The look of the façade varied accordingly. In some, things had happened — in one, something bad: only the orange piers remained, sticking out of smoking rubble. One was naturalistic, abstract, decorative, chromatic, reduced, slap-dash, muddy, thin, thick, pretty, ugly, shallow, deep etc. Only one had figures — a pantheon of heroes and heroines standing around looking baffled, as if beamed from wherever they were, still doing what they had been. In that one, a woman, naked but for white socks and Mary Janes, stood outside a kind of hovel in the museum gardens. All had tongues of flame hovering just above their heads.

"What's the little flame?"

"Pentecost. That's my wife, Cynthia, posing as Chagall's daughter. Her quim is denuded — contra Freud."

She was the woman from the Academy.

Serendipitously, she arrived, her Life Drawing class model in tow.

She looked Tile up and down.

"That explains the strange car."

Tile bowed.

"Perlat Tile, my wife, Cynthia."

"Good morning."

"Good morning."

"I looked for you."

"I looked for you."

"You disappeared."

"I was there."

"So was I."

"Where were you?"

"Where were you?"

"At the bar."

"I was too. I turned around for a second. The next time I looked, you were gone."

"We went downstairs."

"It was crazy, Professor. After The Skipit Club, Ghengis Cohen came on and swallowed a contact microphone. He might as well have stuffed it up his ass! He, he, he had reverb and echo-delay and it was cranked. I'm not kidding! He climbed on a stack, stuck a finger down his throat, and, and, and, and puked. Up it came. The p.a. started to roar. He jumped into the crowd. It blew! Children, children."

DD, Bebe and Kiki came from the back to see who was raving. When they saw, they screamed. The youth picked up one in each arm, swung them around.

"SAUNA!"

"Cool."

Everybody but Dr. and Mrs. Faqu, and Tile, went to partake.

She lit a cigarette and got on a sofa, one leg under her, the other pulled up to her chest. Tile moseyed back into the Dr.'s studio.

He hadn't been looking very long before she strolled in.

"What do you think?"

"I've no idea. I follow a handful of artists working in Florence from the early fourteen-hundreds up to the early fifteen-hundreds."

"Dear me. Who are you again?"

"Sorry, Perlat Tile. Am I too old fashioned?"

"No fashioned. You're the footballer Ali famously saw drinking with Enver."

"At Naj's. Yes. He was on the neighboring stool. I'm not sure what to make of this."

"Ali paints single frame cartoons with no punchlines."

"They don't say something?"

"Something like, 'Dr. Ali Faqu understands, and is an artist of truth', perhaps?"

"What did he paint before?"

"You mean 'before before'?"

"He didn't do this when we were young."

"No. He painted the Secretary meeting hero soldiers, shepherds, and miners. He did the murals at the Ministry of Sport and Culture. Sport was politicized too of course. Were you political?"

"Football had political nuances, when it came to roommates for example."

She laughed.

"I painted too, but was at the Institute. Ali was at the Art Academy."

"That interesting? The Institute?"

"The logic of socialism in one country had its moments."

"You couldn't say it but Lenin's internationalism made better sense to me."

She laughed again. This was going all right.

"I visited the Institute once, with my team. We got Orders of Merit the year we won the league. What did you do there?"

"I analyzed western culture to scientific standards in laboratory conditions."

"What sort of stuff?"

"Political philosophy, fiction, fashion magazines, comics, popular music, tv series, investigated free- and group-sex, smoked hashish, dropped acid, drank Coke, snorted coke. I was a theoretical hippie for the secret police, along with performing other party tricks."

"What about art? How was art viewed?"

"In accordance with the principle that the best of previous social formations shall be preserved — life being transitional. There were arguments of course over the transitivities. We saw pretty much whatever the German gallery system showed. Speaking of seeing — seen enough? Let's sit."

Shrieks came from the back. She sighed, leaned back, eyes distant.

"Was Naj a good trainer?"

"He knew how."

"He does have strong hands. Speaking of knowing, known Enver long?"

"I don't know him. I just met him. What's he to you?"

"We were friends. He attended conferences and symposia at the Institute. We talked art, ran around together, even traveled abroad for a non-aligned socialist youth conference once — to London. He went to all the museums. It was mad. He was supposed to be working artists. He can be funny."

"What'd you do in London?"

"I went to gigs."

"Was he an artist?"

"He talked up ideas in a Conceptual Art vein but never made objects. He published a bit. You knew Naj was a secret policeman? Right?"

"We knew football was a day job."

"'Day job' sounds sexy."

Bebe and Kiki padded in and plopped themselves down. DD came and plunked himself down between them. The three of them shouted in unison as Dr. Ali entered.

"DRINK."

"Of course, my children. And what would you like?"

"No beer; no wine."

"Not even bubbly wine?"

"CHAMPAGNE! YES!"

Dr. Ali left for a moment and returned with a magnum bottle. The cork shot clear across the room. Kiki covered the flood with her mouth. It ran out her nose. She choked and her towel fell down. Dr. Ali's eyes got big. She puffed herself up, watched Cynthia through slit eyes. Ali topped up glasses all around. Bebe showed Kiki a bruise on the inside of her thigh. Kiki poked it. Bebe drew in a sharp breath and glared. Kiki mocked her. Cynthia's young friend waved to her. She waved back. He smiled at Tile, raised his glass. Tile smiled back, went for a piss, then looked out a window into the courtyard. The sun was on his car — the windshield wet with condensation.

He looked at his watch. It was already nine.

Just when he was thinking that he should go home, Cynthia appeared.

"Heading for the day-job, big boy?"

13

Early that evening he was back at Naj's to think and drink on his own. The music wasn't on yet and the joint was practically empty.

How well did Cynthia know Naj? How well did he, really?

He hadn't been at the bar long, staring at himself in the mirror, when the image swung aside with a little bang, and Naj appeared through a hidden door.

He was distracted, almost humming. Whatever he was thinking made him smile.

Tile waited to be noticed.

The barman came over.

"Boss?"

"Make me a Bloody Mary."

"Spicy?"

"Extra."

"Coming up."

"I — Who's that? Hey! Perly boy! Just the man I want to see."

"Naj."

The barman came with his Bloody Mary.

"Cheers."

"Cheers."

They drank. The barman went back to polishing glasses.

Naj beckoned. Tile went around the bar and slipped through the mirror door and followed him back up the passage to a lobby with three doors he'd seen before. One led to his office.

"Come on in. Sit down."

From his jacket pocket he produced a ring of keys with a red plastic corkscrew pendant, and a blued, snub-nose, .38 calibre Smith & Wesson Police Special.

"I want to be ready for trouble."

Sirens howled in the distance.

He put the pistol on the table, took the keys and unlocked a shallow closet lined with shelves filled with rows of binders, assembled the corkscrew, stuck it in a hole at the top of what turned out to be a unit, and twisted.

Orderly penetration was rewarded with a click. He pulled down. The thingy dropped a notch and swung aside easily to reveal a dark room from which he retrieved a hard drive, then reset the unit.

"I was going to call you. That statuette? I may have a clue."

"Wow."

"An old comrade, in prison — still — got stabbed in the neck. He's in the hospital and won't say anything to the cops about who or why. He asked to see me. The cops agreed — I've got a tail. They're probably thinking he wants me to settle the score somehow, or that he told me who might want him dead. There are more than a few. I brought flowers. I had to laugh. A cop bigger than you patted me down. The old boy was hooked up to a stack of monitors, drips and feeds, looking not so good, but, from the eyes, not like dying just yet. He had a sheet of plastic and a felt tip. We had a little back and forth. It was a drug dealer stabbed him — a fight over a boy — but that wasn't the point. He was close to the Hoxhas. He wants out and thinks maybe he's got a bargaining card. Like I told you — word's out about the statuette. He says he's got it and wants to trade it for a deal."

"Man-o-man."

"It was at the Marxist-Leninist Institute. That stuff is now in the National Archive."

"Wow."

"It was funny. To fuck with the cops I said I'd put the flowers in a glass? I went to the basin and began running the water. I said, 'This is too hot. I'll let it run for a minute.' Sure enough, when I came out they were sore, wanted to know if I was trying to flood the place."

"What'd you say?"

"Flowers need water."

"Why the gun?"

"Every player in town will be looking for the statuette."

"Fuck. Maybe I need a gun. And what's the hard-drive for?"

"You shall see, my son."

On the hard drive, in a duplicate file of the inventory of miscellany in the possession of the Institute at the time of its shuttering, they found the list of goods belonging to Naj's old comrade.

He owned all sorts, from a Nazi's skull to Freud's cigar-smoking machine. His collection of hetero- and homosexual pornography was extensive but there was no mention of the statuette as such. The only promising listing said: 'Sculptures (4x)'.

Getting into the National Archive was easy for Naj. But they only found three crates marked 'sculpture', all the same size. One held five small busts — Marx, Engels, Lenin, Stalin, and

Mao. Another held a bronze stag beset by hounds; another, some Roman in marble, missing her nose. The last crate was missing.

He rang Cynthia.

Three quarters of an hour later she slid a black Merc sedan to a smooth stop at the front door of his apartment block. He jumped in.

She was chewing gum, grinning.

"Where to, big boy?"

As they roared towards Pablon's hotel Tile heard a rustling from the backseat. Up popped Ms. Jasmine. She leaned on the back of the seat and smiled.

Mr. Pablon had checked out, leaving no forwarding address. When tempted, for a small consideration, the concierge — an old football fan — remembered his saying something to his friends about the weather in Venice.

They took the next ferry.

Crossing the Adriatic, Cynthia told a story in English

> "One day a chicken came into the public library, and went to the desk. The librarian asked, could he be of help? She clucked — book. He gave her one. She tucked it under a wing, and left. The following day she came again. Again he asked if he could be of help. She clucked twice — book book — was given two books, tucked

them under a wing, and left. Next day she was there again, clucking three times — book book book — was given three books, put them under her wings, and left. This went on for days, the number of books called for increasing by one each day until, at last, nine books in, the librarian had grown so curious he decided that he would follow her if and when she came again. He was happy when she returned the very next day, clucking — book book book book book book book book book book. He gave them to her, and, keeping a safe distance, followed her out, down the library steps, across the road, into the park, down to the lake. There she disappeared behind a stand of reeds. The librarian approached quietly, and parted them. The hen stood on the bank, the fresh stack of books nearby, the forty-five previously loaned adjacent. In the water not far off shore a bullfrog sat on a lily pad. She held one of the new selections up and showed it to him. He blinked, croaked, 'read it', and she put it with the rejects before holding up another."

"You think that's funny?"

"I like it. It can be worked in German too — *buch* being the mother of *book*. There has to be some leeway of course, whatever the language — in English, chickens don't say *book*, they say *cluck*. In German, they say, *pok*. As for 'read it', it would be easy enough to say 'gelesen' and make it sound like a frog said it, though that isn't what frogs say in German, anymore than 'read it' what they say English, which is 'ribbit'. In German, frogs say, *quak* — but for the *c*, very like what ducks say in English."

Santa Maria dei Miracoli (Venice), Pietro Lombardo

14

Once in Venice they visited town hall and checked the death register for burial dates.

Early next morning Tile was under one of three upturned gondolas on a dock outside a boatyard opposite Santa Maria dei Miracoli, the fifteenth century church where Pablon was busy praying over a box that did not contain the ashes of his Albanian cousin.

From the water rose damp chill air smelling of algae, oil, sweet mold. Gray-brown, it rippled lightly. A rat appeared not two meters away, jumped in, disturbing the relative calm, swam across, hopped out, up the short flight of stone steps to the quay of the little church. There it cleaned and preened sympathetically. If you ever saw Disney's *Ratatouille*, you know how charming rats can be.

The guide book reported the little church as having been built by two merchants to give thanks for a miracle in the neighborhood. It was a high box with a rounded lid — looking like an oversize treasure-chest. The box part was divided in two horizontally by a simple architrave, and vertically into five sections by pilasters — 1–1–1.5–1–1 — Ionic above, Corinthian below. There was plenty going on in the spaces — cruciform slits with ornate ends, monochromatic geometric shapes framed in dark molding, rosettes, windows, one big one made up of four ellipses, three times longer than wide, overlapping — like the orbits of electrons around a nucleus. There was statuary here and there too, the main piece being a relief in a shallow pediment above the front door — Mary and the Christ Child. They leaned out, and smiled down.

The back of his neck started to ache.

He returned to watching the water flow.

A bottle passed; a dead ginger cat; a flattened paper cup. All at once the church door opened and there was organ music. The cortège filed out — Pablon, Dr. Giorgio, and Mr. Vari, followed by a pair of hefty attendants in dark suits, wearing black armbands, carrying a box the size of a wine crate, shrouded in black velvet festooned with a laurel wreath.

Instead of the traditional funeral gondola, they loaded it on a motor launch with a black ribbon draped across its bows. It roared to life, backed a bit, and moved off slowly, grumbling, gradually picking up speed, towards the Grand Canal.

Tile emerged from his hiding place and began to run along the quay, towards a side-water where Cynthia and Ms. Jasmine were waiting in a small skiff hired for the occasion. They would follow to the graveyard, spot where the box got put, wait for the sad party to leave, and get the statuette before Pablon and Co. had time to return — probably planned for sometime after dark.

Something snapped though. Rather than proceed to the rendezvous, he caught up with the funeral launch, and launched himself at it from the quay with the idea of 'cutting to the chase', so to say.

Faces onboard widened in universal astound, seeing him soaring. Astound turned to laughter when he fell short.

Pablon waved as they motored away.

His pleasure didn't last long.

At the entrance to the Grand Canal they were intercepted by Venice police in a high-powered launch, their Tirana counterparts having alerted them to irregularities in the export voucher for the ashes. On Tile's view, Naj's handy work.

15

In the late Fifteenth Century interest in the visual arts turned in part on language that a work enabled. Processing didactic pictographic functions had been in place since the end of Ninth Century iconoclasm. As an instrumentality at the service of religion, visual art was a relatively surefire way to convey information without ambiguity. There were illiterates after all, and they too needed to learn. As a secular instrument, the statuette served the taboo it unambiguously broke in life-like, well-rendered detail. The casting was good, and period. There was naturalness to the forms, rightness, proportionality.

In real terms, it was a minor scandal, of historical value but limited public interest. Most of that went to the legal angles. When, in accord with agreements between the Albanians and Italians, the piece was returned to Tirana, press and media begged for photographs, hoping to fan the flame but the authorities kept it under wraps. A few artist's impressions appeared hopefully. The story failed to go viral.

Ms. Jasmine claimed ownership of the statuette, producing a bill of sale from the grandson of Naj's old pal. He claimed that his grandfather had given it to him before he was arrested when the old order fell, and that it had been locked up before he could retrieve it. When asked why he hadn't pursued it before, he said that he had refrained while his grandfather was still incarcerated out of concern that any notoriety on account of the subject matter might prejudice the case for his parole. He believed all would be put right when his grandfather, a patriot and war hero, was finally released. He and Ms. Jasmine appeared on television together, and were rumored to be marrying. Public opinion said they made a nice couple.

The grandson's claim was challenged by lawyers for the old comrade, who also claimed ownership, arguing that the statuette had only ever been stored at the Institute. His goods had been seized illegally. Analysts felt the very idea of its playing a role in getting him released was delusional. When asked about that, the attorney general shrugged. The statuette had been among holdings of the Marxist-Leninist Institute, a body of the former state. Nine points of the law said it belonged to Albania. Hearings were yet to be scheduled.

Cynthia Faqu enjoyed tabloid celebrity for a moment, speaking on the Institute and her pursuits there. A publisher encouraged her to write her memoirs. Her husband's work got splashed in the press but not much more came of it.

Dr. Harmoni published a text in a German art magazine where he argued that the statuette was not by Antonio or Piero del Pollaiuolo, rather a former apprentice whose name he was researching. He claimed the statuette for Art, for Freedom, for Love.

Pablon & Co. were charged *in absentia* with stealing a national treasure. Their lawyers managed to have the charge reduced to exporting goods under false premises when they agreed to a fat fine and never returning to Albania. The Italians had charged them with importing pornography but quietly let the matter drop in view of the deal with the Albanians and to limit the scandal. The ashes that Pablon had bought had never left the country. Those were returned to the family.

Jumping in the canal added to Tile's fame at Naj's, and to his notoriety at the Chrome Exchange.

Appendix

Tile's Antonio Pollaiuolo files:

E. H. Gombrich, *The Story of Art*, London (1950)

EHG: Renaissance sections, *Story of Art*: "The Conquest of Reality (Brunelleschi, Masaccio, Donatello, Sluter, Jan van Eyck, Witz, Nanni); Tradition and Innovation: Italy (Alberti, Ghiberti, Fra Angelico, Gherardo, Uccello, Gozzoli, Mantegna, Piero, Pollaiuolo, Boticelli, a popular engraving); Tradition and Innovation: the North (Lochner, Tavernier, Fouquet, van der Goes, van der Weyden, Stoss, Schongauer, Colombe) and Harmony Attained (Bramante, Verrocchio, Leonardo, Ghirlandajo, Michelangelo, Perugino, Raphael)."

EHG: Petrarch, *SoA* (pp. 161–2) "Giotto was a contemporary of the great Florentine poet Dante, who mentions him in his 'Divine Comedy'. Simone Martini [...] was a friend of Petrarch, the greatest Italian poet of the next generation. Petrarch's fame today rests mainly on the many love-sonnets he wrote for Laura. We know from them that Simone Martini painted a portrait of Laura which Petrarch treasured. We remember that portraits in our sense had not existed during the Middle Ages and that artists were content to use any conventional figure of a man or woman, and to write on it the name of the person it was intended to represent. Unfortunately, Simone Martini's portrait of Laura is lost, and we do not know how far it was a real likeness. We do know, however, that this artist and other masters of the fourteenth century painted likenesses from nature, and that the art of portraiture developed during that period. Perhaps the way in which Simone Martini looked at nature and observed details had something to do with this, for the artists of Europe had ample opportunity of learning from his achievements. Like Petrarch himself, Simone Martini spent many years at the court of the Pope, which was at that time not in Rome but in Avignon in southern France. France was still the center of Europe, and French ideas and styles had a great influence everywhere."

EHG: early Renaissance in Florence, *SoA* (pp. 167–9): "The word 'renaissance' means rebirth or revival, and the idea of such a rebirth had gained ground in Italy ever since the time of Giotto. When people of the period wanted to praise a poet or an artist, they said that his work was as good as that of the ancients. Giotto had been exalted in this way as a master who had led to a true revival or art; by this, people meant that his art was as good as that of the famous masters whose work they found praised in the ancient writers of Greece and Rome. It is not surprising that this idea became popular in Italy. The Italians were very much aware of the fact that in the distant past Italy, with Rome her capital, had been the centre of the civilized world, and that her power and glory had waned since the Germanic tribes, Goths and Vandals, had invaded the country and broken up the Roman Empire. The idea of a rebirth was closely connected in the minds of the Italians with the idea of a rebirth of 'the grandeur that was Rome'. The period between the classical age, to which they looked back with pride, and the new era of rebirth for which they hoped was merely a sad interlude, 'The Time Between'. Thus the idea of a rebirth or renaissance was responsible for the idea that the intervening period was a Middle Age — and we still use this terminology. Since the Italians blamed the Goths for the downfall of the Roman Empire, they began to speak of the art of this intervening period as Gothic, by which they meant barbaric — much as we speak of vandalism when we refer to the useless destruction of beautiful things. ¶ We now know that these ideas of the Italians had little basis in fact. They were, at best, a crude and much simplified picture of the actual course of events. We have seen that some seven hundred years separated the Goths from the rise of the art that we now call Gothic. We also know that the revival of art, after the shock and turmoil of the Dark Ages, came gradually and that the Gothic period itself saw this revival getting into its full stride. Possibly we can understand the reason why the Italians were less aware of this gradual growth and unfolding of art than the people living farther north. We have seen that they lagged behind during part of the Middle Ages, so that the new achievements of Giotto came to them as a tremendous innovation, a rebirth of all that was noble and great in art. The Italians of the fourteenth century believed that art, science and scholarship had flourished in the classical period, that all these things had been almost destroyed by the northern barbarians and that it was for them to help revive the glorious past and thus bring about a new era. ¶ In no city was this feeling of confidence and hope more intense that in the wealthy merchant city of Florence, the city of Dante and of Giotto. It was there, in the first decades of the fifteenth century, that a group of artists deliberately set out to create a new art and to break with the ideas of the past."

EHG: A. Pollaiuolo, *SoA* (p. 196–8): "While these and other artists [Brunelleschi, Donatello, Alberti, Ghiberti, Fra Angelico, Uccello, Mantegna, Piero della Francesca] were applying the inventions of the great generation of Florentine masters, artists in Florence became increasingly aware of the new problems that these inventions had created. In the first flush of triumph, they may have thought that the discovery of perspective and the study of nature could solve all difficulties which are presented. But we must not forget that art is altogether different from science. The artist's means, his technical devices, can be developed, but art itself can hardly be said to progress in the way in which science progresses. Each discovery in one direction creates a new difficulty somewhere else. We remember that medieval painters were unaware of the rules of correct draughtmanship, but that this very shortcoming enabled them to distribute their figures over the picture in any way they liked in order to create a perfect pattern. The twelfth-century illustrated calendar [...], or the thirteenth-century relief of the 'Death of the Virgin' [...], are examples of this skill. Even fourteenth-century painters like Simone Martini [...] were still able to arrange their figures so that they formed a lucid design on the ground of gold. As soon as the new concept of making the picture a mirror of reality was adopted, this question of how to arrange the figures was no longer so easy to solve. In reality figures do not group themselves harmoniously, nor do they stand out clearly against a neutral background. In other words, there was a danger that the new power of the artist would ruin his most precious gift of creating a pleasing and satisfying whole. The problem was particularly serious where big altar-paintings and similar tasks confronted the artist. These paintings had to be seen from afar and had to fit into the architectural framework of the whole church. Moreover, they had to present the sacred story to the worshipers in a clear and impressive outline. [...] Antonio Pollaiuolo, 'The martyrdom of St Sebastian'. Altar-painting, 1475. London, National Gallery shows the way in which a Florentine artist of the second half of the fifteenth century, Antonio Pollaiuolo (1432?–98), tried to solve this new problem of making a picture both accurate in draughtmanship and harmonious in composition. It is one of the first attempts of its kind to solve this question, not by tact and instinct alone, but by the application of definite rules. It may not be an altogether successful attempt, nor is it a very attractive picture, but it clearly shows how deliberately the Florentine artists set about it. The picture represents the martyrdom of St Sebastian, who is tied to a stake while six executioners are grouped around him. This group forms a very regular pattern in the form of a steep triangle. Each executioner on one side is matched by a similar figure on the other side. ¶ The arrangement, in fact, is so clear and symmetrical as to be almost too rigid. The painter was obviously aware of this drawback and tried to introduce some variety. One of the executioners bending down to adjust his crossbow is seen from in front, the corresponding figure from behind and the same with the shooting figures. In this simple way, the painter endeavoured to relieve the rigid symmetry of the composition and to introduce a sense of movement and counter-movement very much as in a piece of music. In Pollaiuolo's picture this device is still used rather self-consciously and his composition looks somewhat like an exercise. We can imagine that he used the same model, seen from different sides, for the corresponding figures, and we feel that his pride in his mastery of the muscles and movements has almost made him forget the true subject of his picture. Moreover, Pollaiuolo was hardly quite successful in what he set out to do. It is true that he applied the new art of perspective to a wonderful vista of the Tuscan landscape in the background, but the main theme and the background do not really blend. There is no path from the hill in the foreground on which the martyrdom is enacted to the scenery behind. One almost wonders whether Pollaiuolo would not have done better to place his composition against something like a neutral golden background, but one soon realizes that this expedient was barred to him. Such vigorous and lifelike figures would look out of place on a golden background. Once art had chosen the path of vying with nature, there was no turning back. Pollaiuolo's picture shows the kind of problem that artists of the fifteenth century must have discussed in their studios. It was by finding a solution to this problem that Italian art reached its greatest heights a generation later."

EHG describes how artists such as Pollaiuolo developed geometrical devices that accorded with the rules of the recently developed system of perspective, mastered representation of the phenomenology of light and dark, and developed "the space of the stage." He pooh-poohs the idea that this (or any) systematicness could ever be or lead to anything like scientific progress in art, no matter how much Pollaiuolo or anyone else operated "not by tact and instinct alone," but "applying definite rules," "working out of the cumulative knowledge of the day."

EHG: Pollaiuolo's role in northern analysis, *SoA* (p. 209–10): "Another great northern artist who went to Rome (for a pilgrimage in 1450) was Rogier van der Weyden (1400?–64). Very little is known about this master except that he enjoyed great fame and lived in the southern Netherlands, where Jan van Eyck had also worked. [...'The Descent'] shows a large altar-painting which represents the descent from the Cross. We see that Rogier, like Jan van Eyck, could faithfully reproduce every detail, every hair and every stitch. Nevertheless, his picture does not represent a real scene. He has placed his figures on a kind of shallow stage against a neutral background. Remembering Pollaiuolo's problems, we can appreciate the wisdom of Rogier's decision. He, too, had to make a large altar-painting to be seen from afar, and had to display the sacred theme to the faithful in the church. It had to be clear in outline, and satisfying as a pattern. Rogier's picture fulfils these requirements without looking forced and self-conscious as does Pollaiuolo's. The body of Christ, which is turned full face towards the beholder, forms the centre of the composition.

The weeping women frame it on both sides. St John bending forward, like St Mary Magdalene on the other side, tries in vain to support the fainting Virgin, whose movement corresponds to that of Christ's descending body. The calm bearing of the old men forms an effective foil to the expressive gestures of the principal actors. For they really seem like actors in a mystery play or in a tableau vivant grouped or posed by an inspired producer who had studied the great works of the medieval past and wanted to imitate them in his own medium. In this way, by translating the main ideas of Gothic art into the new, lifelike style. Rogier did a great service to northern art. He saved much of the tradition of lucid design that might otherwise have been lost under the impact of van Eyck's discoveries [p. 203, oil-painting and 'how to make a picture a mirror of nature by carefully adding detail upon detail until the whole fame was filled with painstaking observation']. Henceforward northern artists tried, each in his own way, to reconcile the new demands on art with its old religious purpose."

EHG: Pollaiuolo's role in discussion of Leonardo, *SoA* (p. 224–6): "By a singular misfortune, the few works which Leonardo did complete in his mature years have come down to us in a very bad state of preservation. Thus when we look at what remains of Leonardo's famous wall painting of 'The Last Supper' [...] we must try to imagine how it may have appeared to the monks for whom it was painted. The painting covers one wall of an oblong hall that was used as a refectory by the monks of the monastery of Santa Maria delle Grazie in Milan. One must visualize what it was like when the painting was uncovered, and when, side by side with the long tables of the monks, there appeared the table of Christ and his apostles. Never before had the sacred episode appeared so close and so lifelike. It was as if another hall had been added to theirs, in which the Last Supper had assumed tangible form. How clear the light fell on the table, and how it added roundness and solidity to the figures. Perhaps the monks were first struck by the truth to nature with which all details were portrayed, the dishes on the tablecloth, and the folds of the draperies. Then, as now, works of art were often judged by laymen according to their degree of lifelikeness. But that can only have been the first reaction. Once they had sufficiently admired this extraordinary illusion of reality, the monks would turn to the way in which Leonardo had presented the biblical story. There was nothing in this work that resembled older representations of the same theme. In these traditional versions, the apostles were seen sitting quietly at the table in a row — only Judas being segregated from the rest — while Christ was calmly dispensing the Sacrament. The new picture was very different from any of these paintings. There was drama in it, and excitement. Leonardo, like Giotto before him, had gone back to the text of the Scriptures, and had striven to visualize what it must have been like when Christ said, "'Verily I say unto you, that one of you shall betray me', and they were exceeding sorrowful and began every one of them to say unto him, 'Lord, is it I'" (Matthew xxvi. 21–2). The gospel of St John adds that 'Now there was leaning on Jesus' bosom one of his disciples, whom Jesus loved. Simon Peter therefore beckoned to him, that he should ask who it should be of whom he spake.' (John xiii. 23–4). It is this questioning and beckoning that brings movement into the scene. Christ has just spoken the tragic words, and those on His side shrink back in terror as they hear the revelation. Some seem to protest their love and innocence, others gravely to dispute whom the Lord may have meant, others again seem to look to Him for an explanation of what He has said. St Peter, most impetuous of all, rushes towards St John, who inadvertently pushes Judas forward. Judas is not segregated from the rest, and yet he seems isolated. He alone does not gesticulate and question. He bends forward and looks up in suspicion or anger, a dramatic contrast to the figure of Christ sitting calm and resigned amidst this surging turmoil. One wonders how long it took the first spectators to realize the consummate art by which all this dramatic movement was controlled. Despite the excitement which Christ's words have caused, there is nothing chaotic in the picture. The twelve apostles seem to fall quite naturally into four groups of three, linked to each other by gestures and movements. There is so much order in this variety, and so much variety in this order, that one can never quite exhaust the harmonious interplay of movement and answering movement. Perhaps we can only fully appreciate Leonardo's achievement in this composition if we think back to the problem we discussed in the description of Pollaiuolo's 'St Sebastian'. We remember how artists of that generation had struggled to combine the demands of realism with that of design. We remember how rigid and artificial Pollaiuolo's solution of this problem looked to us. Leonardo, who was little younger than Pollaiuolo, had solved it with apparent ease. If one forgets for a moment what the scene represents, one can still enjoy the beautiful pattern formed by the figures. The composition seems to have that effortless balance and harmony which it had in Gothic paintings, and which artists like Rogier van der Weyden and Botticelli, each in his own way, had tried to recapture for art. But Leonardo did not find it necessary to sacrifice correctness of drawing, or accuracy of observation, to the demands of a satisfying outline. If one forgets the beauty of the composition, one suddenly feels confronted with a piece of reality as convincing and striking as any we saw in the works of Masaccio or Donatello. And even this achievement hardly touches upon the true greatness of the work. For, beyond such technical matters as composition and draughtmanship, we must admire Leonardo's deep insight into the behaviour and reactions of men, and the power of imagination which enabled him to put the scene before our eyes. An eye-witness tells us that he often saw Leonardo at work on 'The Last Supper'. He would get on to the scaffolding and stand there for whole days with folded arms just looking critically at what he had done before painting another stroke. It is the result of this thought that he has bequeathed to us, and, even in its ruined state, 'The Last Supper' remains one of the great miracles wrought by human genius."

EHG: Pollaiuolo's role in discussion of Raphael, *SoA* (p. 240–45): "This applies to a smaller fresco ['The nymph Galatea', ca. 1514, Rome.] which Raphael painted in the villa (now called the Farnesina) of a rich banker, Agostino Chigi.

As subject he chose a verse from a poem by the Florentine Angelo Poliziano which had also helped to inspire Botticelli's 'Birth of Venus'. These lines describe how the clumsy giant Polyphemus sings a love song to the fair sea-nymph Galatea and how she rides across the waves in a chariot drawn by two dolphins, laughing at his uncouth song, while the gay company of other sea-gods and nymphs is milling round her. Raphael's fresco shows Galatea with her gay companions. The picture of the giant was to appear elsewhere in the hall. However long one looks at this lovely and cheerful picture, one will always discover new beauties in its rich and intricate composition. Every figure seems to correspond to some other figure, every movement to answer a counter-movement. We have observed this method in Pollaiuolo's showpiece. But how rigid and dull his solution looks in comparison with Raphael's! To start with the small boys with Cupid's bows and arrows who aim at the heart of the nymph: not only do those to right and left echo each other's movements but the boy swimming beside the chariot corresponds to the one flying at the top of the picture. It is the same with the group of sea-gods which seem to be 'wheeling' round the nymph. There are two on the margins, who blow on their sea-shells, and two pairs in front and behind, who are making love to each other. But what is more admirable is that all these diverse movements are somehow reflected and taken up in the figure of Galatea herself. Her chariot had been driving from left to right with her veil blowing backwards, but, hearing the strange love song, she turns round and smiles, and all the lines in the picture, from the love-god's arrows to the reins she holds, converge on her beautiful face in the very centre of the picture. By these artistic means Raphael has achieved constant movement throughout the picture, without letting it become restless or unbalanced. It is for this supreme mastery of arranging his figures, this consummate skill in composition, that artists have admired Raphael ever since. Just as Michelangelo was found to have reached the highest peak in the mastery of the human body, Raphael was seen to have accomplished what the older generation had striven so hard to achieve: the perfect and harmonious composition of freely moving figures."

EHG: Leonardo, Michelangelo, Raphael, were paradigms; 'Last Supper' the last word on drama, 'Galatea' perfect composition. The case for both was made off Pollaiuolo's 'St Sebastain' — recall how EHG characterized 'SS' as a "not altogether successful," "not very attractive" "attempt" to solve the problem how to make a big altar-painting that fit the architecture of the church, how it showed what happened, reconciling accurate draughtsmanship and harmonious composition? How Massaccio's version of the same event more plainly exemplified what we understand as Renaissance mastery?

H. W. Janson, *History of Art*, London (1962)

HWJ (p. 426–7): "The popularity of portrait busts after about 1450 suggests a demand for works to be shown in the homes of individual art patrons. The collecting of sculpture, widely practiced in ancient times, apparently ceased during the Middle Ages; the taste of kings and feudal lords — those who could afford to collect for personal pleasure — ran to gems, jewelry, goldsmith's work, illuminated manuscripts, and precious fabrics. The habit was reestablished in fifteenth-century Italy as an aspect of the 'revival of antiquity.' Humanists and artists first collected ancient sculpture, especially small bronzes [...] which were numerous and of convenient size; long before contemporary artists began to cater to the spreading vogue, with portrait busts and with small bronzes of their own 'in the manner of the ancients'. ¶ A particularly fine piece of this kind is by Antonio de Pollaiuolo (1431–1498), who represents a sculptural style very different from that of the marble carvers we discussed above. Trained as a goldsmith and metalworker, probably in the Ghiberti workshop, he was deeply impressed by the late styles of Donatello and Castagno, as well as by ancient art. From these sources, he evolved the distinctive manner that appears in our 'Hercules and Antæus' (fig. 584) [ca. 1475. Bronze, height 18" (with base). National Museum, Florence]. To create a free-standing group of two figures in violent struggle, even on a small scale, was a daring idea in itself; even more astonishing is the way Pollaiuolo has endowed his composition with a centrifugal impulse: limbs seem to radiate in every direction from a common center, and we see the full complexity of their movements only when we turn the statuette before our eyes. Despite its strenuous action, the group is in perfect balance. To stress the central axis, Pollaiuolo, as it were, grafted the upper part of Antæus onto the lower part of his adversary. ¶ There is no precedent for this design among earlier statuary groups of any size, ancient or Renaissance; our artist has simply given a third dimension to a composition from the field of drawing or painting. He himself was a painter and engraver as well as a bronze sculptor, and we know that about 1465 he did a large picture of Hercules and Antæus, now lost, for the Medici Palace (our statuette also belonged to the Medici). ¶ Few of his paintings have survived, and only a single engraving, the 'Battle of Ten Naked Men' [...]. This print, however, is of great importance, since it represents Pollaiuolo's most elaborate pictorial design. Its subject — undoubtedly a classical one — has not yet been convincingly identified, but that matter is not so significant; the primary purpose of the engraving, obviously, was to display Pollaiuolo's mastery of the nude body in action. About 1465–70, when the print must have been produced, this was still a novel problem, and Pollaiuolo contributed more than any other master to its solution. An interest in movement, coupled with slender proportions and an emphasis on outline rather than on modeling, had been seen in (Andrea del) Castagno's 'David', for example [...], who in these respects is clearly the progenitor of the 'Ten Naked Men'. Pollaiuolo also drew upon the action poses he found in certain types of ancient painted vases [...]. But he realized that a full understanding of bodily movements demands a detailed knowledge of anatomy, down to the last muscle and sinew. ¶ All of these ten naked men do indeed have an oddly 'flayed' appearance, as if their skin had been stripped off to reveal the play of muscles underneath, and so, to a somewhat lesser degree, do the two figures of our statuette. Equally novel are their facial expressions, as strained as the bodily movements. We have already encountered contorted features in the work of Donatello and Masaccio [...] but the anguish they convey does not arise from, or accompany, the extreme physical action of Pollaiuolo's struggling nudes."

HWJ: "International Style somehow became outmoded; its hegemony broken. In Italy the break took the form of 'classical revivals' — but this time expressed in and as realistic imitation of nature. In the north, a new level of order was introduced in the pursuit of truth to nature. Artists were transformed from manual laborers into theoretical practitioners."

HWJ: "With the change in the status of his work, the artist's outlook, too, underwent changes. Now in the company of scholars and poets, he himself often became a man of learning and literary culture; he might write poems, an autobiography, or theoretical treatises. As another consequence of this new social status, artists tended to develop into one of two contrasting personality types: the man of the world, self-controlled, polished, at ease in aristocratic society; and the solitary genius, secretive, idiosyncratic, subject to fits of melancholy, and likely to be in conflict with his patrons. It is remarkable how soon this modern view of art and artists became a living reality in the Florence of the Early Renaissance."

Palazzo Medici (Florence), Michelozzo di Bartolomeo

Prologue

"To Sig. Guido Bidoni, Workshop, Arno Street. January 15th, inst. Bidoni, greetings. Happy New Year. A little project? You will have seen the Hercules and Antæus I commissioned? I am inspired to commission something along similar lines but an entirely different tale from our city's hero's adventures. Come see me? Friday? At 3? L."

The palace was begun in 1444. Brunelleschi was still alive. The Medici wisely rejected his late, grandiose, 'Roman style'. Michelozzo's comparatively modest design reflected the Medici's appreciation of a rising mood of asceticism. Without being a Brunelleschi fortress — a staple of old Florence — it recalled the great man's principles, compressed in three stories graded and constituted of distinctive materials — roughhewn masonry topped by smooth, rusticated blocks topped by a single smooth surface crowned by a cornice in a Roman temple style.

The meeting had been brief. What Il Magnifico had in mind was culturally Greek, and risqué — for him as artist, tricky.

He sketched in broad lines what had been spelled out in graphic detail.

His wife admired the drawing.

"Hercules is like you. Who is the boy?"

He had replied that it wasn't him, and 'the boy' was nobody. Both came out of his imagination. What was she intimating? If anything?

It was nothing.

She pointed out several things about him, features and stances that he was unable to deny were similar to Hercules'. Well? She arched an eyebrow.

He replied that he had remarked how, sometimes, when one drew a human figure spontaneously from imagination, what materialized, sometimes, did have hints of oneself. Did that mean such images were self-portraits?

She smiled and shrugged. What did she know? Going on appearances?

One more thing, but for the member, the boy reminded her of herself without a bosom.

That floored him.

"Lorenzo will turn you over in his mind, and us."

He groaned and vowed silently to expunge any gestalt of himself or hint of her from what he finally presented, knowing full well that only took care of the visual half the problem.

How could one blind a mind's eye to something all but visible?

His wife's observations weighed heavily. The material implications of the image of the man's looking something like him and sex with a fantasy boy were clear enough, and, although he had developed what he felt was an argument for the femininity of the swooning figure based on a positive reading of the negative image of the 'male', he feared it might be turned against him by some clever twist on the part of his wife that he could not think of, so kept quiet, ruing lascivious imagining.

Carnival came and went. Traditional apocalyptic abandon, laxity, and heightened sexuality, abjectly realized.

Ash Wednesday morning, nursing hangovers, he and his wife went to Church and received ashes. Back home they inspected the smudges on their foreheads — '*memento mori*' — a priest's thumbprint, palm ash on human skin.

He had been mentally paralyzed. Every image seemed bound to be tied to him and his wife. Pure simulacra changed nothing. Then, he found what he prayed to God was a solution: give the figures the faces of known people!

He made Hercules after Pollaiuolo's, and the boy became the King of France.

His wife was impressed.

> "Not bad. And not merely anatomically, but politically correct."

PICTURE CREDITS

Cover
Referee image
© ljupco/123RF Stock Photo

Page 3
Hercules and Antæus
Photo by Sailko and is licensed
under CC BY 2.5

Page 48
Antonio del Pollaiuolo; Piero del Pollaiuolo,
The Martyrdom of Saint Sebastian
© The National Gallery, London.

Page 50
Leonardo da Vinci
The Last Supper
Public Domain

Page 51
Raphael
Triumph of Galatea
Public Domain

Page 88
Santa Maria Dei Miracoli Church in Venice
© Pstedrak / Dreamstime.com
Public Domain

Page 114
"The Palazzo Medici Riccardi in Florence"
© George Tatge for Alinari Archives/Getty Images

Art, Mystery
has been printed in a limited edition
of 800 hardcover copies.

The book has been designed in the United States — in Chicago, Illinois, and Los Angeles, California — by author Mayo Thompson, graphic designer Dan Osborn, and record conglomerate Drag City (Incorporated).

It has been printed on 45# Alternative Natural Offset paper from Resolute Forest Products of Montréal, Quebec, Canada, with printing and binding capably handled in October of 2017 by Bang Printing of Brainerd, Minnesota.

The text of this book has been set in Garamond Premier Pro, designed by Robert Slimbach and released in 2005 by Adobe Systems Incorporated of San Jose, California. The roman characters are based on Claude Garamond's original hand-cut masters from the mid-1500s, while the italic characters, as is common with Garamond type, are based on an italic type by Garamond's contemporary, Robert Granjon.

Chapter titles are set in Helvetica Neue, produced by Linotype-Hell AG, now known as Monotype GmbH, located in Bad Homburg, Germany. It is a reworking of Helvetica, which was introduced in 1957 by Max Miedinger and Eduard Hoffmann of the Haas Type Foundry in Münchenstein, Switzerland.